Max's Midnight Swirl

by Jane Brandi Johnson

Illustrated by Lisa Bohart

Imagination will take you everywhere!

Enjoy!

 Graphic design by Lisa Bohart. Illustrations by Lisa Bohart.

Edited by Jane Brandi Johnson

Library of Congress Control Number: 2014903715

Printed in the U.S.A.
Printed by CreateSpace, Charleston, SC

Printed April 2014

For our youngest dreamers ...

Evan, Carlee, Sadie, Liam, Lily, and AJ

With my face on the pillow, all ready for bed,
a fantastic idea drifts into my head.

A sky full of
animals ...
if you know what I mean!

With scoops and dips and swirls of ice cream!

It's a sporty-fun day.

Just look at the crowd!

And try not to laugh.

Shhh! ... at least not out loud!

It's Turtle the skater, Wolf on a pole,
and Shrimp shooting arrows ...

What a sight to behold!

Would you believe?

Five snails on a run!

And a hurdling pig ...

It's just too much fun!

Look!
In the clouds!
Three goats in a boat!

And tennis-pro hamsters?
Well that gets MY vote !

Rat and Porcupine race through the sky.

I'm beginning to laugh ... but I just don't know why!

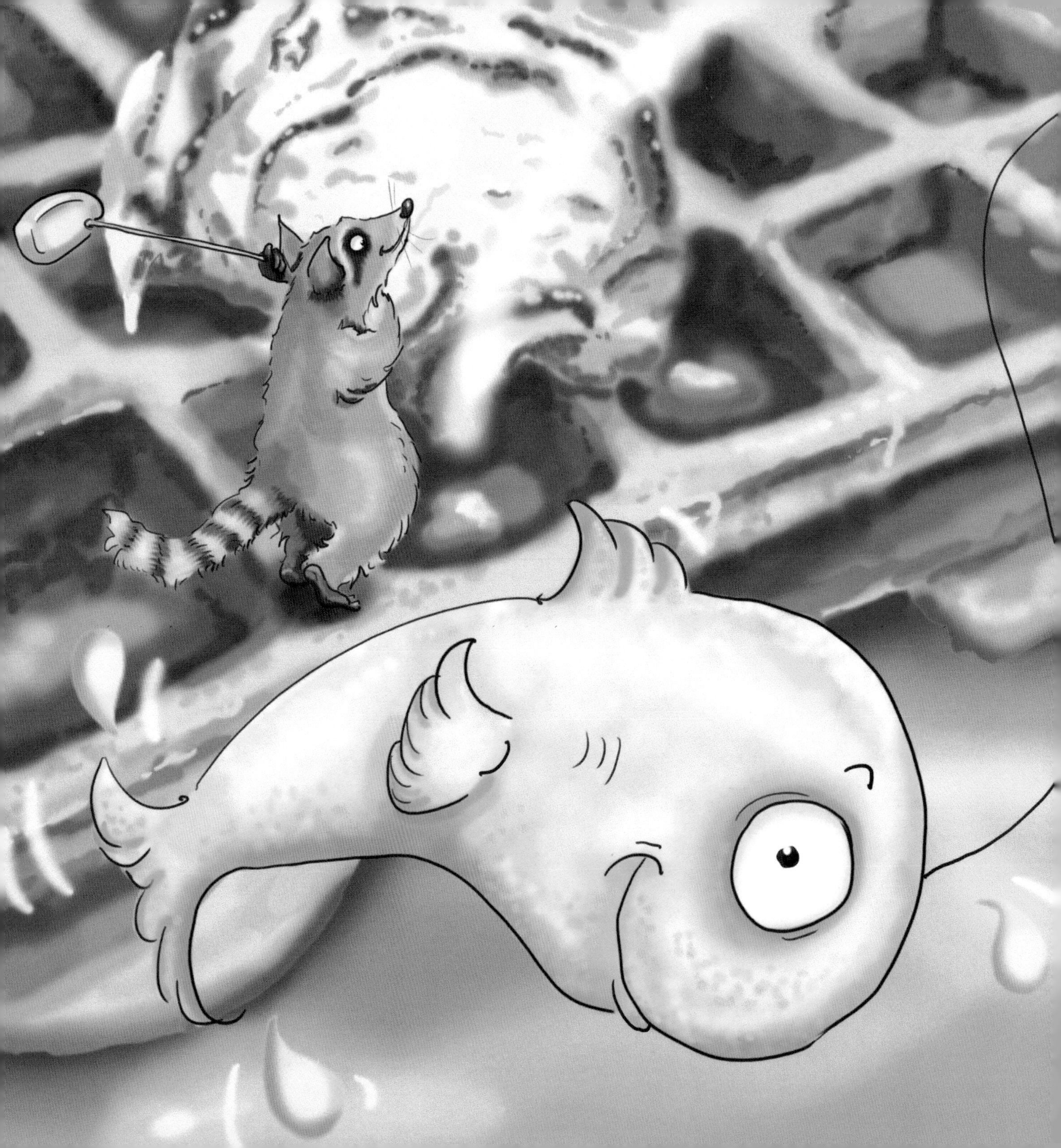

A black and white dog ...What a fishing machine!
And a golfing raccoon just rounds out the scene!

Mouse in her tutu ...

She's the belle of the ball!

And Camel on high dive ...

Oh, don't let him fall!

Anteater swings on gymnastic rings,

as Elephant juggles SIX scoops of ice cream!

A fencing red fox, a sandcastle cat,
and a fierce little badger with a pineapple hat!

Goose skis down an icy cream slope.

It's vanilla, strawberry and chocolate ... I hope!

A rabbit equestrian, a bear playing pool.
I'm almost awake now ... and starting to drool!

I like all the sports
and the animals, too!

It feels like a swirl of games at a zoo!

But what I love MOST is the yummy ice cream!
so ... PLEASE!

Don't wake me up from this

Fabulous Dream!

rrring!

Made in the USA
Charleston, SC
12 May 2014